A SOUND OF SWANS FLYING

by

Lucille and James Horner

BOOK ONE

NO SUCH LAUREATE EARTH?

SYNOPSIS

Historical drama. This novel traces the experience of two families, one English and one South African, who are fated, despite geographical distance, to be intertwined from the beginning of the twentieth century until the present. From birth and childhood onwards, through sibling rivalry, love, ambition, loss, war, migration, endeavour, vanity, rejection, tragedy, travel, romance, civil unrest, innovation, idealism, racial issues, humour, cultural controversies, language differences, disputes over inheritance, divorce, fostering, step-families, introversion and existentialism, the characters search for ways to live, even to succeed. They must deal with the quickly changing circumstances of their time. Most significantly they must survive the indecipherable enigma that is South Africa.

Available in electronic and paper versions.

CHAPTER ONE

VYGIE

by

Lucille Horner

For

Oscar

DISCLAIMER

This is a work of fiction. The story, the incidents described and the names and characters of persons in the story all originated in the writer's mind and are not based on actual people or events. Any resemblance of characters in this fiction to persons living or dead is purely coincidental. Opinions expressed by the fictitious characters are the opinions of the fictitious characters, not the opinions of the author.

ISBN: 9798404918182

DRAMATIS PERSONAE

BELT THE REVEREND	Missionary, acquaintance of Henry 'Graph' Middler
MIDDLER HENRY ('GRAPH') 1883 TO 1961	Father of Natalie. Nicknamed 'Graph' for his fascination with telegraphs and communications generally. Of Scottish descent.
MIDDLER HESTER (nee CALITZ) 1900 TO 1979	Mother of Natalie. Plattelander (i.e. a lady who spent her entire life on the veld or living in 'dorps') (villages). Ultra conservative without knowing it. Of Dutch descent.
MIDDLER ANASTASIA	Eldest daughter of Henry and Hester
MIDDLER BELINDA	Second daughter of Henry and Hester
MIDDLER CHARLENE	Third daughter of Henry and Hester
MIDDLER NATALIE	Fourth daughter of Henry and Hester
MIDDLERS, OTHER CHILDREN	Delaine, Yvette, Frederic, Gavin and Garth
VAN MIDDEL LEONARD (LEN) 1881 TO 1957	Slave descendant. Man-servant to the Middler family. Of mixed Malay, Bushman, Hottentot and European blood.
VAN MIDDEL NAANIE 1881 TO 1961	Wife of Len. Slave descendant. Maid-servant to the Middler family. Of mixed Malay, Hottentot and European blood.

1918 TO 1933 OUDTSHOORN, CAPE PROVINCE,

UNION OF SOUTH AFRICA

VYGIE (Afrikaans for Mesembryanthemum)

"Dis 'n mooi meisiekind, mies," ("It's a pretty girl-child, madam,") Naanie said as she carefully placed the tiny being on the receiving blanket.

The night's labour had been long. But now, in the glimmer of a lantern supplemented by first light, Naanie, servant and midwife, made steady progress.

"Nie te lank nou nie," ("Not too long now,") she said after a while to the newly-delivered mother. No stranger to the exigencies of childbirth, Naanie was still deeply engrossed in her work.

The minutes ticked by. Hester lay exhausted. In the haze of loveliness that attends the beginning of life she listened to her child's first cries.

Concentrating intently, Naanie severed the umbilical cord.

Still damp-haired and sweat-strewn, Hester longed to look for the first time into the face of her baby.

Naanie worked diligently on. But then, at last, just as Hester summoned the energy to rearrange the pillows and sit up, Naanie swathed the child in a soft robe, gathered her up and lowered her into Hester's arms.

"Baie mooi!" Naanie said, ("Very pretty,") a smile of satisfaction on her prematurely-aged Hottentot-Malay face.

"Hallo, Natalie," Hester said to her child.

Natalie, the wild rose, quick in thought and limb, was the fourth daughter. She had five sisters and three brothers. By virtue, it seemed to her, of the order of their birth, her brothers and sisters always attracted more parental attention than herself.

To compensate for parental preoccupation, Natalie resorted, early in life, to grand gestures and shock tactics. But this response, instead of bringing the recognition she sought, earned the disapproval of her siblings.

"Agh, Natalie is such a show-off," Charlene, the third-eldest sister, would remark.

"She needs to be taught manners," Belinda, the second-eldest, agreed.

Yet, beyond her immediate family, Natalie, even in her very early years, had friends. Her protection of the underdog, her loyalty in adversity, her flashes of insight and merriment, all were qualities that earned trust, made her one in whom the worried and sad chose to confide. Those who knew her well were drawn to a part of her being seldom seen by her family, an attractive world of inner peace in which, away from sibling rivalry, she was able richly to give and richly receive.

Loving her as they did, Natalie's friends accepted her eccentricities and defended her from her deep anxieties. Profoundly aware, the mothers in the neighbourhood discussed her attributes.

"Die kind het 'n spesiale intelligensie," ("That child has a special intelligence,") one would say.

"Ander stel haar uit," ("Others defer to her,") another would agree.

"Maar ek kyk met stilte ontsteltenis," ("But I watch with silent dismay,") a third would add, "Sy is so soet en kwesbaar dat sy soms gewond raak deur die spontaniteit van haar eie persoonlikheid." ("She is so sweet and vulnerable that she is sometimes wounded by the spontaneity of her own personality.")

"Ons mense het 'n plig om sterk te word in ons wereld," ("Our people have a duty to grow up strong in our world,") a fourth would comment disapprovingly. "Ons s'n is nie 'n wereld waarin swakheid geduld kan word nie." ("Ours is not a world in which weakness can be tolerated.")

Whatever parents and siblings might think, Natalie believed in the openness of her own heart. "I must always be kind to people, no matter what happens," she often said to herself. "I must be the best."

In her small home town of Oudtshoorn in The Cape Province, the name given at Union in 1910 to the country formerly known as The Cape of Good Hope Colony, Natalie Middler set about proving and improving herself.

"You are a thinker, aren't you Natalie," her father, Henry 'Graph' Middler, would sometimes say. He was aware of struggles rather too deep for one so young. "My Vygie," he said, using his pet name for this daughter, "is always on the lookout for fine things of the mind and for greatness of the heart, isn't she?" He looked on his offspring with kindness.

Natalie longed to rise above the taunts of siblings, to demonstrate to her family and to the world that she, Natalie, could be self-sufficient. "I must be able to stand alone," she would say to herself, "but in a friendly way that earns respect."

But her youthful efforts met with scant success. Busy parents left the child largely to her own devices. The world of the nineteen thirties had great things on its mind and ignored her flamboyance. Natalie used the vacuum to further her quest.

"Youth is even briefer than Life," she said to a school friend. "We *must* use it. We *must* find things we *really* want to do. We must *search*."

Music was important. She went fortnightly to the house of the Norwegian, Mrs Haugen, for piano lessons.

"Agh, Natalie can't hear anything else when she's playing the piano," Belinda complained waspishly.

"You are right," Charlene agreed. "You think she is ignoring you. But she isn't really. She just doesn't answer you because her tiny skull is full of sound."

Natalie frequently sat for hours at the piano in the lounge. On Thursday afternoons at the neighbouring church she would sit unobserved in the semi-darkness of the pews, listening to the organist practising. When she heard the servants rehearsing for their choral competitions, she wandered off to their quarters to listen. On Saturdays their singing might last all afternoon and half the night.

Graph was seated in the lounge one evening, reading his newspaper while Natalie played his gramophone. "People," she said to her father, "have strong feelings about music."

"People hold surprisingly strong views about many things," Graph replied looking at her with interest over the top of the page. "Music is an expression of culture."

For the most part Natalie kept her search for self-confidence to herself. It was a painful loneliness, this exploration, but the self-censorship brought dividends. Her father was her confidante.

"Listening to music is like reading a book, isn't it Daddy?" she asked. "You have to listen to each note like you have to understand each word of a book."

"Yes, I suppose you do," Graph looked at her, intrigued.

"People think about their feelings when they listen to music, don't they?"

"Yes, I suppose they do," Graph agreed once more.

"And, often when they listen to music they are longing for something to happen, aren't they, Daddy. Or they are feeling sad about the past."

"Yes. Thinking sadly about good things that happened in the past is called 'nostalgia'. Do you know that word, Vygie? Nostalgia. It's a good one to know."

"Oh, well, everyone has something to be sad about," Natalie said.

"Yes, I suppose they do," Graph agreed once more, wondering at the conversation.

"But it is not always good to talk about the things you love, is it Daddy?" Natalie searched for confirmation.

"Well......," Graph replied slowly, "it is important always to think about the consequences of your words."

"Daddy, please may I have a gramophone for my birthday?" she asked.

"Whatever for?" Graph asked. "Isn't mine good enough for you? You use it often enough. You've been listening to my Mozart KV 466 concerto all afternoon."

"Yours needs a new needle," she said.

"Len," Naanie said percipiently to her husband, "hier kom nou weer die meisietjie." ("Len, here comes the little girl again.") It was 1927. Leonard van Middel was in his forties. He was of a similar racial mix to his wife. Both had wizened faces and woolly hair.

It was most unusual for any white person, let alone a very young girl-child, to enter the sparse world of the servants' dwellings but Natalie at nine years of age, with her long-flowing jet-black hair, her finely embroidered, predominantly white dresses and her Roman nose, had been visiting for some time. She was sweetly drawn to the uniquely local music rising through the searing, motionless air.

At the very moment Natalie walked around the corner of the building that screened the master's house from the desert-yellow sparsity of the servants' courtyard, Graph was seated in his well-appointed lounge entertaining a missionary newly arrived from

England. "No doubt," Graph was saying defensively to The Reverend Belt, "harsh social injustices exist elsewhere in South Africa, and out in the huge world beyond. But in the household of Henry 'Graph' Middler unkindness is banned. Acceptance of racial differences is not just second-nature to my family, it is ingrained. In fact we delight in these things. And the delight is reciprocated. Especially by our servants. But not only by our servants. In fact, all who know us are aware of our ways. Mind you, there are those amongst our own people who dislike our stance. But locally, our attitude is well known."

"Well, howsoever you make your case," The Reverend Belt opined testily, "it must be an exception that proves the rule."

"Of course there are regrettable lapses," Graph continued, "but in our home family and servants alike hold for the most part to the fair-minded example set by my forebears. Inevitably, in our daily lives, comparisons of a racial and a social nature are often made. Sometimes such comparisons produce uproarious mirth. Both sides enjoy the hilarity. Both sides are amused by one-another's characteristics, by the racial and cultural differences. But mutual respect is under-written.........By me. I try to foresee trouble and take steps to prevent conflict. My sincere wish is to make life pleasant for everyone. Wherever possible."

"But, compared to your good-humoured and long-suffering servants," said The Reverend Belt, "you are a rich man. You have education, land and money. In these things your servants can never hope to compete with you and the truth is that in the economic and political circumstances of South Africa they have little choice but to defer to you."

"In that, South Africa is no different to other countries," Graph replied. "The servants are free to leave us if they don't like us. The forebears of my servants had long been slaves in the service of the Middler family. When the British Empire outlawed slavery, my servant's ancestors were bemused. They had nowhere to go with their new-found freedom, little to offer. Their skills were limited to the menial work of slaves. They had been slaves for generations. There had never been any contact with the Dutch East Indies homes from which some of their ancestors had been pressed into slavery. There had been generations of racial inter-mixing and at times, complete social breakdown. In reality their origins were beyond their ken, almost beyond their imagination. My ancestor, Charles Middler, the head of the family and the slave-owner at the time of emancipation was not an unkind man. When he told his slaves they were free to go and that he could not afford to pay them for their work, they asked to be allowed to stay. And he agreed. As life in The Cape of Good Hope improved and times changed, my family began to pay wages to their freed slaves. Generation followed generation. A natural order of existence stood and was understood. Lives were closely shared. Respectful acknowledgement by Middlers and Van Middels of one-another's births, christenings, marriages and funerals ran parallel to a clear divide of race and status. The world set the parameters, the families conformed."

"Maybe," said The Reverend Belt. "But I cannot believe that was or is a general pattern."

"In fact Van Middel, the family name of the servants, is simply an adoptive form of Middler," Graph added tenaciously.

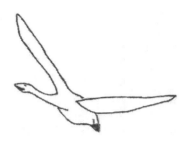

So, on that Saturday afternoon in 1927, Len Van Middel was seated in his usual Saturday afternoon place, on a rickety chair in a shady but bare-earthed corner of the quadrangle around which the drab servants' quarters were built. And as usual, he was passing the time singing a song of his own composition on a lute of his own making.

"Hallo," Natalie said, greeting Naanie, her gathering of female friends and their pastorale of mixed-race children as she turned the corner into the quadrangle. Natalie was too young to have any notion that by visiting the servants she was once again breaching invisible divides. It never occurred to her to contrast her middle-class life with the relative penury of the servants. The racial divide did not alarm her. She had always known and accepted the disparities. But the bare-footed coloured children suspended their play for a few long moments and stood looking at her. Unconcerned, the child, her polished black shoes shining in the sunlight, seated herself cross-legged before Len on the hard earth and with her chin resting on her palms, stared attentively upwards at him as he sang and played. By her silent, attentive audience, Natalie struck up a substantial affinity with musicians she met, whatever the place, whatever the genre of music.

Len's status as a poor man-servant was no barrier to this special relationship.

Observing with sudden happiness that the young mistress had yet again innocently arrived to listen to his songs, Len gave her a small secret smile that did not in the slightest interrupt his playing. He was rewarded with a tiny smile in return. In his plain, clean family space, from his place in the shade, he continued his song with studied normality. It was a long song. Involuntarily, he was now playing for the sunlit child seated in her spotless white dress on the dusty earth before him, and his artistry took on fine precision.

So flattered was Len by Natalie's interest that he briefly contemplated asking if the child could accompany Naanie and himself when they went to choir practices at their church in the location. But he instantly dismissed the idea as unthinkable.

"Naanie, please may I have something to drink," Natalie asked when Len's song had reached its end. Before Naanie could respond she continued, "Leonard, please sing us another song. Sing vir ons die een van '*die volstruis en haar eier*'," ("Sing us the one about '*the ostrich and her egg*'"). Natalie's unaffected directing of the servants, even in their own quarters, was accepted without question. No-one found anything offensive in it, the more so since Natalie was so young, so well versed in their ways, so trusting of them and so natural with them. It was the way things were, had always been.

Had it not been for this profound status quo and for the generations of trust between the Middlers and the Van Middels, connotations of ugly suspicion and fear might have entered the equation. The servants might have feared white man's outrage. *"A white girl-child alone in the servants quarters?" "Nooit!" ("Never!")* As it was, however, all present were at their ease. It was a remarkable matter, simple and innocent.

In the lounge at the big house the political sparring continued. "In some ways our families are better neighbours to one another than are the average families in your English city terraced row," Graph was saying to The Reverend Belt. "We have the advantage of not being so crowded one on top of another as are the people in England. We have more space and yet we are closer. For example, Naanie van Middel was the midwife at the birth of all my children. Neither family," Graph continued "give thought to any other way of living. We all are happy.

There are not many trouble-makers. The racial divide is merely part of the order and decorum of it all. Native South Africans of every colour, up and down the country, recognise the pattern. Households of the Middler kind are not some ubiquitous imperial harmony. But they are, in South Africa, an everyday occurrence."

Down in the servants' quadrangle, Len began the song about the ostrich and her egg. Natalie listened with all the solemnity of the very young. She was a child of many dreams. But at that moment in the refined long-gone peace of 1927 the sweetly brocaded nine-year old could not for a moment have imagined that eight decades hence she would still summon up Len's music of the desert. She would still hear his song from that long-gone afternoon, wonder at its loss, wonder at the complete disappearance of the world into which they had all been born.

Naanie went momentarily into the dark interior of her house and re-emerged wearing her servants cap and apron. "Ek gaan maar net a bietjie Webb's lemonade kry," ("I am going to fetch some Webb's lemonade,") she said to Len and her friends. "Wil jy 'n koekie hê Nattie?" ("Would you like a biscuit, Nattie?")

"Yes please, Naanie," Natalie replied in the matter-of-fact, ultra-polite manner of her upbringing and her class.

At the gate, bidding farewell to The Reverend Belt, Graph was still elaborating. "We are all completely bilingual," he said. Both families mix English and Afrikaans in their everyday speech, as the subject and tenor require."

"I thought your wife spoke Dutch," said The Reverend Belt. "And that Afrikaans was for those Boer types who live in remote districts and are more out of touch with civilisation."

"No, we are more Afrikaans by nature, I think," said Graph sensing in The Reverend Belt the not uncommon English antipathy for Boers. "Our family ancestry is English, Scottish, Dutch, German and French in more or less equal parts."

"Oh, I see," The Reverend Belt replied. "I should think Dutch is a higher language and culture than Afrikaans, shouldn't you?"

Graph bristled. But, with his wife, Hester, in mind, he did not wish to fall out with a minister of religion. And with his take on history in mind he did not relish any engagement in a conversation about colonists and republicans, Dutch and Afrikaans. He knew such a conversation would inevitably drift into the contentious subjects of demographics and The

Boer War. And so Graph chose a simple comment as the way out. "Sometimes," he said, "Afrikaans provides an idiom that serves the moment, sometimes English more nearly expresses a concept. This mixing of languages is more marital and geographic than hierarchical. The white Middler family do however, as a product of their education and culture, utilise a greater vocabulary in both languages than do, for example, the Van Middels. In deference to origins, I am usually addressed in English by my wife and I usually address my wife in her home language, Afrikaans. Mind you, perhaps she still thinks of her home language as Dutch, I am not sure. But for the most part, the conversation will continue in the language in which it began. We think of our shared languages as a kind of wealth."

"Do you?" The Reverend Belt said looking at his pocket watch with a superior air. "I must be off," he said, impatient to leave.

"Drop in for coffee any time," Graph said. He shook hands with The Reverend Belt. "You will find that dropping-in is the norm in South Africa. We do not stand on the ceremony of invitations. As the English do. We just drop in, you see. You will always be very welcome. At any time. That is our way."

Working on a Saturday afternoon?" Graph asked curiously when, a few minutes after The Reverend Belt had left, Naanie unfastened the lower stable door to the kitchen and came into the main house. Without waiting for an answer he asked, "Have you seen Nattie? The child seems to have disappeared again."

"No, Baas (Boss)," Naanie replied in her deep Cape Coloured accent, "the child is safe. She is visiting us. So I've come to pour her a juice and fetch her a biscuit."

"Oh!" Graph said. He paused for a silent moment, smiling with amused perplexity, his forehead wrinkling into a frown. "She is visiting you," he said kindly. "Of course." It was a revelation. Scratching his balding pate he moved seamlessly on to exchange a few thoughts with Naanie about the orchard, the egg-gathering and the biltong.

Graph allowed a good three quarters of an hour to pass before he went to the servants' area.

"Hallo Leonard. Just come to check on my daughter," he said as he turned the corner into the servants' quadrangle.

The coloured children once more stopped their playing and stood staring.

Even the adults were silent now, listening, taking note.

"Afternoon Baas," Len said. "She is fine." He gestured at Natalie as he arose in greeting.

Natalie jumped up and climbed instantly into the adored and adoring arms of her father.

"And what are you up to, my child?" Graph asked lovingly but with a hint of concern.

Len was standing now.

"I am listening to Leonard, Daddy. He plays such lovely music. His songs are so lovely. He makes them up all by himself, you know. And he plays his guitar so well. And he *made* his guitar. Please will you stay and listen with me while Leonard sings some more."

"Well……ummm," Graph began.

"Please, Daddy," the child implored.

"Well……….ummmm…………but ……….," Graph began again.

"*Please*, Daddy," the child insisted.

"But maybe, Leonard doesn't feel like singing to us.............," Graph countered. Even, however, as he spoke, Naanie placed an old dining-room chair next to him. Graph recognised the chair as one Hester had long since discarded from the main house.

The proffered chair was rather rickety. Graph seated himself gingerly. With Natalie on his knee, a line of laundry drying to one side and the smell of wood-smoke, both fresh and stale, all around, Graph prepared to listen. Len took up his rough-hewn instrument and struck the opening notes of his next song.

It was a very long song, mostly in a vernacular mixture of English and Afrikaans with here and there a Hottentot or Xhosa word and a click sound interspersed. Graph roughly followed its ancient tale of Bushmen rustlers attacking Hottentot kraals (homesteads), committing murder and being driven off. In time the crimes were avenged when the Bushmen died under the poisoned arrows of the Hottentots.

Quite soon a group of coloured children had seated themselves on the ground around Graph and Natalie. Len felt his musical skill being pushed to the limit as he endeavoured to deliver entertainment to an unexpectedly attentive, unusually large audience. Even Naanie's friends, the mothers and fathers of the assembled children, paused, stopped their conversations and stood around to watch and listen.

There followed another song about the effect on the harvest of fire and flood and about the effect on the harvesters of burnt wine. And then there was a song about tribes and clans, about Xhosa and Sotho, Fingo, Pondo, Thembo, Griqua and white men, about the desert and the unimaginable splendour of distant Cape Town which very few of those present had actually seen, and about the ocean which was also merely hearsay to most of that company. Lastly Len sang of wild animals and the dangers they posed to livestock, and about how the livestock must inevitably sometimes be slaughtered for feasts. And about ceremonies, feasts and clannish variations in feasting customs.

From her seat on her father's knee, Natalie followed Len's songs avidly, as did everyone else now that "die baas" (the boss) had come to listen. It was the music of those in whose company she had, in infancy, come to consciousness and whose conversation she had always known. The genre was not new to her and her fresh mind was open to and versed in the folklore of it all.

But Graph, interested though he could not help being, secretly thought it all inferior. "Oh Lord," he said to himself, "there are so many things demanding my attention and I must sit here."

Concealing his longing to leave and wondering how he might extricate himself and his daughter in a way that seemed natural, Graph stayed on. He must humour his child and defer to 'the labour'. "What a primitive jingle-jangle this music is," he said to himself. He had lived much longer than his sweet daughter, seen more, knew the ropes and the pitfalls. There was a status to maintain. He felt uncomfortable with this level of fraternisation, did not wish to set any precedent.

Soon enough, at exactly the right moment, Graph did leave. Taking great care that it was not too soon, he watched for a natural opportunity and when one came he arose, courteously thanked Len and Naanie for their hospitality, nodded to the gathering, and, with daughter in hand, disappeared around that same corner by which he had arrived. A few steps and he was back home in his grand house.

After that day Natalie's visits to hear Len's playing dwindled. But they did not altogether cease. And then, after a reflective interval they became more frequent again. Yet even as she began returning to the music in the dusty courtyard of the servant quarters, an awareness was developing. There were, she noted, complexities in her birthright. Steadily, through everyday life, she imbibed the full significance of the many social divides into which she had been born. Through her father's example she discovered and meditated on his view that the white people were a fine and lonely elite. Also, there were his words. "Never forget that you are a *white* girl, Vygie," Graph said. "You must *be* the better person you are. *All* white people must be. You can *never* allow standards to slip. *No* white person can."

This parental insistence brought back to Natalie's mind, passages from her favourite book, Sir Percy Fitzpatrick's 'Jock of The Bushveld', which Graph had given her as a birthday present.

"Like Sir Percy Fitzpatrick," Natalie said.

"Yes. Like Sir Percy," Graph agreed.

"How many times have you read that book now, Vygie?" Graph asked one day. He noted how Natalie, sitting squeezed into his armchair beside him, ran her finger lovingly over the marginal illustrations of 'Jock of The Bushveld'.

"Many times," she answered wistfully. "I think I know the first page almost off by heart."

"Ah yes," Graph understood at once. "Those first few pages go to the very heart of loneliness. Such a compelling piece of writing."

"Daddy," she asked, looking at him and still touching a picture of a shield and an assegai on the open book, "is Zululand a colony on its own?"

"No," Graph answered, "it used to be, but it was annexed to Natal. It has been part of Natal for many years now."

"What does annexed mean?" she asked.

"Sort of joined up and taken over," he replied.

"Why was it annexed?" she asked, and there was unmistakable concern in her voice.

"Who knows?" Graph answered. "Some cost-saving reason I expect. These things normally are. But why," he asked, noting her disquiet, "would such a thing worry you?"

"Sir Percy liked the Zulus, don't you think, Daddy?" she asked by way of an answer.

"He certainly did," Graph answered with an uncertain smile. "Especially he liked that drunken savage of a manservant of his, one Jim Makokela, of whom you have no doubt been reading," Graph looked closely at his daughter.

"Oh, Jim was such a *funny* native," Natalie enthused. "I especially like the way Jim didn't like Sam because Sam read the bible. Don't you love him, Daddy?"

Graph laughed. "I don't think Jim could find it in his heart to like any black man who wasn't a Zulu," he said. "Perhaps not being a Zulu was, to Jim's mind, Sam's major shortcoming."

"But isn't it terrible," Natalie lamented, "how Jim said he would kill Sir Percy if the Zulu king ordered him to. And he said it at the very same time as he said he knew Sir Percy had saved him and been a good boss."

"Oh yes," Graph agreed. "Jim Makokela is amusing. But he is also tangible evidence that the Zulu fighting spirit is very much alive. For even though we subdued the Zulus such a long time ago, they would, given half a chance, still be happy to kill every white man and every animal that we have, and burn down all our houses. They are savages! Jim Makokela and his tribe are the epitome of everything that civilization will always have to worry about. But..........."Graph pulled himself up, "you are too young to worry about all that yet." He looked at Natalie, stroked her hair, reflecting with pleasure at the depth of her responses to the written word.

Natalie was too anxious about the subject to let it go. Her fresh mind had obviously been contemplating the enormity of the threat.

"So how can we be friends with the Zulus if they want to kill us?" she asked.

Graph stared at his daughter. "We have to offer them friendship but be always very much on guard," he replied.

"Perhaps we should give them back Zululand as their own place to rule?" she suggested. "Then they wouldn't need to kill everybody else because they would have a place of their own?"

"Good heavens, Vygie! That book has really stirred some worries in you, hasn't it?" Graph gathered her in for a fatherly hug. "I don't really have answers to your questions, my child. All I can say to you is that if each one of us always does his very best, then that is all that can be done. And," he added after a few moments of embracing her, "*I* shall always look after you. So you needn't worry about it all. My sweet girl."

Graph thought for a moment. "And in a way, we have given them their own land, haven't we? That's what the tribal reserves are, aren't they?"

"Sir Percy Fitzpatrick loved the veld in a special way, didn't he daddy?" Natalie persevered.

"Well, yes," Graph hesitated. "In 'Jock of The Bushveld' he certainly loved the lands he passed through...............But there were other books he wrote in which you see other things...........you see ....more of him,...........you see..........perhaps........ a different kind of Sir Percy........."

"What other things?" Natalie asked.

"Well..............., for instance," Graph suggested, "in a book he wrote called 'The Transvaal From Within', you may, with hindsight, wonder about and

question his reasoning..........
But......... you don't want to read that
yet...........it is far too political and
difficult for you."

"Well," said Natalie thoughtfully, "Sir
Percy thinks we all have to be very
clever and very kind and very brave
and very strong in order to stay in
charge. Except. He doesn't actually
say that. But you know that is what he
really means."

Kindness was not the major attribute of the response of the older sisters to the information that Natalie had once more been a guest in the servants' quarters. Anastasia, Belinda and Charlene Middler seized on a moment when the adults were out shopping, to deride Natalie for her non-conformity.

They cornered Natalie in her bedroom. "So," Anastasia began the amusement. "You have been visiting the servants again!"

"Even though we have often told you not to," Belinda added forcefully.

"Don't you know your place?" Charlene smirked down at the surprised Natalie who in silent terror held close the cloth doll she had never really outgrown and stared wide-eyed up at the towering aggressors.

"What colour are you?" Belinda demanded haughtily, pressing home the attack while Natalie still puzzled over their words.

Natalie stared at Belinda bemused.

"What is the colour of your skin?" Belinda insisted.

"White," came an almost inaudible, uncomprehending reply.

"And what colour are the servants?" Belinda sneered.

"They are coloured," Natalie said in pale terror. She would have preferred to remain silent but she feared that failure to answer would result in physical aggression.

"White people don't mix with coloureds or blacks, do you hear?"

Belinda bent forwards. Face to face with Natalie, her eyes drilled menacingly into Natalie's eyes.

"Do you hear?" Belinda repeated, raising her voice.

"Yes," Natalie answered, overawed.

"What do you think you were doing there?" the precocious Charlene demanded. "Who do you think you are? Who do you think *we* are that we would allow a sister of ours to go *there*?"

"I was listening to Len's playing and singing," Natalie answered tearfully but with a sudden lift in her voice as she broke instinctively into fatalistic defiance. This was not the first time she had been subjected to sibling pressure. And yet it always came as a surprise. She would have to learn to prepare for it.

"Well, you are not to go there, see," Belinda commanded as she took hold of Natalie's arm and began twisting. Natalie erupted in all-out resistance shouting and crying and kicking and biting and calling for help.

For some moments she was pinned down and roughly handled by Belinda and Charlene.

Anastasia's young brow furrowed and her stomach muscles tightened. She suddenly re-evaluated the circumstances. Fearing parental disapproval she called a halt to the bullying. She doubted Belinda's motives. She jibbed at Charlene's intensity. She had not meant it to turn so nasty. She wondered how she would reply if Graph learnt of the episode. As eldest she had, after all, been left in loco parentis.

"Okay, stop this," she said in a loud voice.

"Belinda, that is much too wreed! (cruel)!" she insisted.

"Charlene, hou op! (stop it!)"

"Natalie needs to be taught a lesson," Belinda answered venomously.

"Yes, she definitely does," Charlene agreed.

"Yes, But daddy left me in charge and now you have hurt her," Anastasia said determinedly.   She   looked apprehensively at Natalie huddling in the corner of her room and holding a bruised arm.

"What am I going to say to daddy about this?"

Natalie, now trembling violently and overwhelmed by tears, remained defiant. "I am going to tell daddy everything. *Everything*," she sobbed and shouted at the same time.

Charlene raised a fist to pummel Natalie again but Anastasia caught the raised arm and screamed at her, "Charlene, stop it! Now!"

That night, in the lounge, Graph did notice the bruising on Natalie's arm.

"Goodness, what have you done to your arm, Vygie?" he asked. He walked over to her, lifted her arm and studied the blue and black patches.

Noticing that Natalie winced in pain and was fearful he persevered. "Tell me," he gently demanded, looking into her face, an eyebrow raised.

The full truth came out.

"Come with me, all four of you," he said leading the girls into the privacy of his office.

With Belinda, Charlene and Natalie standing by, Graph rebuked Anastasia.

"I expected more from you, Anastasia," he said somewhat acidly. "You are old enough to understand. I trusted you. I left you in charge. It was up to you to stop this happening."

"And as for you two, Belinda and Charlene, you also ought to know better by now. This home is a haven of peace. Do you understand? None of us can take tranquillity for granted. To preserve serenity there is much that must be constantly tended. You girls have a good life. To have any hope of maintaining your position you have to be constantly decent in everything you do. Most especially, you should care for one another. You are sisters after all. Are you not?"

"Now, all three of you apologise to Natalie and to me and do not let this happen again," Graph said sternly, hoping that his stance was sufficiently strong.

Anastasia and Charlene were crestfallen and mumbled their apologies. But Belinda stood deeply sullen, for between her and Natalie there had always been competition for paternal praise.

Graph kept Belinda back, but dismissed the others.

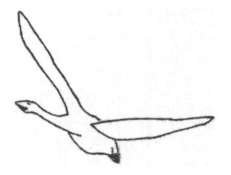

Hester Middler, the girls' mother, played no part in this interlude. Her mind was fully engaged on another matter that had, for all too long, been of great concern to her.

Graph's constancy in directing the Middler family, his ability to deliver the blessing of reasoned normality, was shortly to be painfully tested.

Something destructive, an acute menace, was making its way towards them all.

REQUEST

Dear Reader,

If you have found anything of interest in this chapter, please leave a review on Amazon. Your thoughts will be studied. This is the first of 83 planned chapters. There is a race under way. Will the book be finished before it's time for the crematorium? Your review might just help me to give up 'my day job' so that I win the race.

Thank you.
Lucille H.

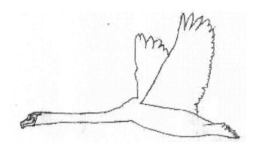

NOTES

NOTES

NOTES

NOTES

NOTES

NOTES

Printed in Great Britain
by Amazon

76697489R00052